PUFFIN BOOKS
UK | USA | Canada | Ireland | Australia
India | New Zealand | South Africa

Puffin Books is part of the Penguin Random House group of companies
whose addresses can be found at global.penguinrandomhouse.com.

www.penguin.co.uk          www.puffin.co.uk          www.ladybird.co.uk

Penguin
Random House
UK

First published in Great Britain 2024
001
Copyright © Frederick Warne & Co. Ltd, 2024
Peter Rabbit™ & Beatrix Potter™ Frederick Warne & Co.
Frederick Warne & Co. is the owner of all rights, copyrights and
trademarks in the Beatrix Potter character names and illustrations

Printed in China

The authorized representative in the EEA is Penguin Random House Ireland,
Morrison Chambers, 32 Nassau Street, Dublin D02 YH68

A CIP catalogue record for this book is available from the British Library

978-0-241-69961-4

All correspondence to:
Puffin Books
Penguin Random House Children's One Embassy Gardens,
8 Viaduct Gardens, London, SW11 7BW

# I LOVE YOU,
## Best Friend

*Every*
# DAY
## THAT

WE
PLAY
together,

IT'S

*always*

FUN,

whatever

THE

WEATHER.

WE LIKE
TO
share

OUR
*games*
AND
TOYS,

To
**RUN**
AND
*jump*

*and*
# MAKE
*some*
# NOISE!

IF
I am
SAD

or

feeling

FEARFUL,

You
LIFT
me
UP

AND
MAKE
ME
cheerful.

When
WE
fall
OUT,

it's
NOT
FOR
long,

THE
*bond*
WE
HAVE

IS *very* STRONG.

I
# TRUST
*you*

AND

*you*

TRUST

ME,

*a*
*friend*
CAN
BE.

Thank you

FOR

BEING

SO

# KIND

AND

*funny.*

When
I'M
with YOU,

I'M A
*joyful*
BUNNY!